THE ZAK FILES

By Sebastian Belle

A GOLDEN BOOK • NEW YORK

ISBN: 978-0-375-85936-6
www.randomhouse.com/kids
MANUFACTURED IN CHINA
10 9 8 7 6 5 4 3 2 1

ZAK - FISKERTON

I'm **Zak Saturday,** and along with my family, I search for wild, weird creatures called cryptids. Luckily for me, I have this really cool power that allows me to control cryptids and a multifunction weapon I call the Claw to help me focus my power!

My family gets into a lot of dangerous situations, and that's why I'm glad to have a superstrong, superagile cryptid like **Fiskerton** watching my back. Fiskerton is like my furry gorilla-cat brother!

My dad, **Doc Saturday,** leads all our missions. He's a scientific genius who has invented tons of high-tech stuff, like our airship and his Battle Glove.

The lady swinging the flaming Tibetan Fire Sword is **Drew Saturday,** my mom. Her sword can cut through almost anything. She's also an ace pilot!

DOC SATURDAY - DREW SATURDAY

DOYLE · KOMODO · ZON

Doyle is my uncle. He's a freelance adventurer who does everything with style.

Komodo is like the family dog, if you think a hungry, mutated Komodo Dragon makes a good pet.

When I want to take to the sky, my own private pterosaur, Zon, flies me wherever I want to go. She and Komodo have saved me more than once when the cryptid-hunting turned dangerous!

THE BAD GUYS

MUNYA - V. V. ARGOST

Most cryptids aren't intentionally bad, but there are a lot of people who are rotten to the core. **V. V. Argost** wants to use cryptids to rule the world! And his henchman, **Munya**, can turn into a big spiderlike thing and spit sticky webbing. (Trust me, it's gross.)

Leonidas Van Rook and **Abbey Grey** are mercenary cryptid hunters who will capture cryptids for anybody willing to pay them enough to do the dirty work.

Agent Epsilon and his son, **Francis**, aren't exactly bad guys, but they never seem to be up to anything good, either! Francis is my own personal archenemy.

VAN ROOK - ABBEY GREY - AGENT EPSILON - FRANCIS

CRYPTIDS

AMAROKS

Amaroks have big fangs, long claws, bad breath, and lots of drool. These hairy cryptids travel in packs and look a lot like werewolves. Always hungry, they'll eat just about anything—including you and me! Amaroks protect sacred Inuit burial mounds in the Arctic, so I guess they're not all bad.

The **Bishopville Lizardman** is half man and half reptile, with scaly skin and long claws. Plus, he can spit some really wicked metal-melting acid!

The **Honey Island Swamp Monster** has big crablike claws and has been known to eat livestock.

BISHOPVILLE LIZARDMAN - HONEY ISLAND SWAMP MONSTER

Nagas are the reptilian servants of the ancient cryptid known as Kur, who is destined to take over the world. As it turns out, I am Kur. (It's a long story.) But since I have no interest in taking over the world, I've had more than a few fights with the Nagas.

NAGAS

Talk about strange eating habits. I get indigestion just thinking about these three flying cryptids!

The **Devil's Cave Bird** drinks blood like a vampire bat.

The **Duah** lures its mates to an undersea nest and eats them!

The **Owlman** uses its hypnotic powers to force people to offer it human sacrifices! Yuck!

BILOKO - RAKSHASA

The **Biloko** looks like a big baboon with a nasty set of wild-boar's tusks. As you can see, it's part primate, part crocodile, and all bad attitude!

The **Rakshasa** is like a really, really big tiger—that can sprout an extra head and an extra set of sharp-clawed feet!

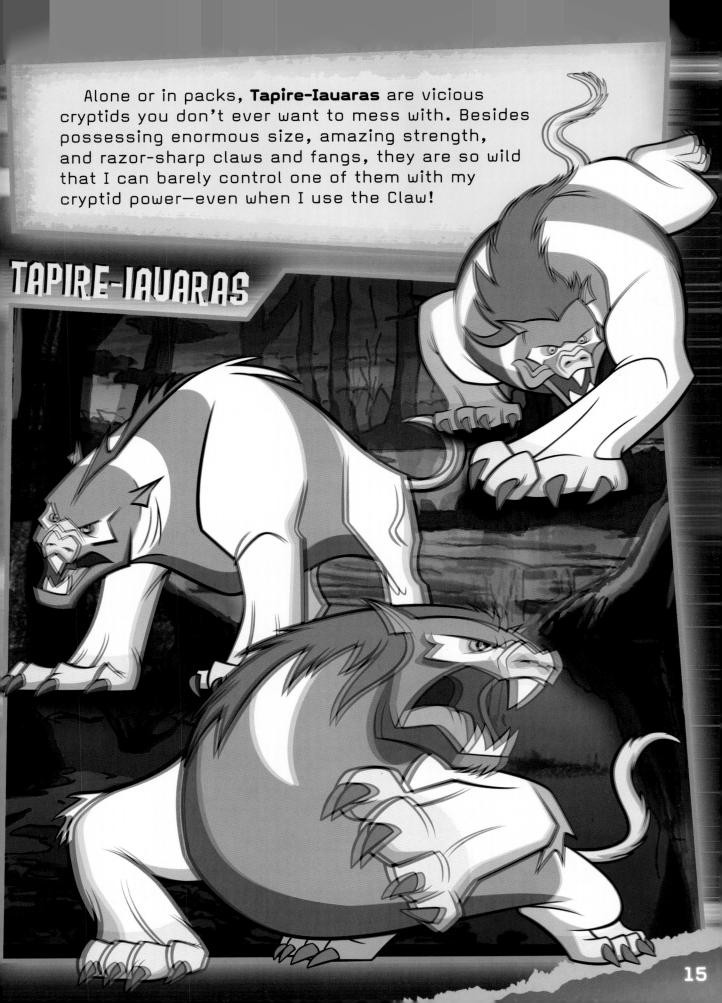

Alone or in packs, **Tapire-Iauaras** are vicious cryptids you don't ever want to mess with. Besides possessing enormous size, amazing strength, and razor-sharp claws and fangs, they are so wild that I can barely control one of them with my cryptid power—even when I use the Claw!

TAPIRE-IAUARAS

The **Alkali Lake Monster** has a vicious horn on the end of its nose and an odor far more powerful than its ferocious snapping jaws. It is one of the biggest aquatic cryptids in the world . . . except for the Kumari Sea Serpent.

ALKALI LAKE MONSTER